the adventures of Jeremy Levi

the adventures of JEREMY LEVI

by
Yaffa Ganz

illustrations by
Harvey Klineman

FELDHEIM PUBLISHERS
Jerusalem / New York

First published 1981
Second, revised edition 1985
Third printing 1989
Hardcover edition: ISBN 0-87306-319-8

Copyright © 1981, 1985 by
Yaffa Ganz

All rights reserved. No part of this publication may be translated, reproduced, stored in a retrieval system or transmitted, in any form or by any means, electronic, mechanical, photocopying, recording or otherwise, without permission in writing from the publishers.

**Library of Congress
Cataloging-in-Publication Data**

Ganz, Yaffa
  The adventures of Jeremy Levi.

  Summary: Relates the amusing misadventures of eleven-year-old Jeremy Levi whose clever ideas always lead to trouble.
  1. [Jews—United States—Fiction]   I. Klineman, Harvey, ill.   II. Title.
  PZ7.G1537Ad   1985   [Fic]   88-31110
  ISBN 0-87306-319-8 (U.S.)

Philipp Feldheim Inc.
200 Airport Executive Park
Spring Valley, NY 10977

Feldheim Publishers Ltd.
POB 6525 / Jerusalem, Israel

Printed in Israel

To **Akiva** נ״י

whose efforts in
Torah and *derech eretz*
are bearing fruit
as he successfully meets
the challenge of growing up

יהי חלקך בתורה ומצוות

contents

I, Jeremy Levi	9
The Livyatan and the O.S.C.	16
Lashon Hakodesh and Judy's Wedding	25
The Klezmerim	34
The J & S Employment Agency	42
Running the House	50
Zeidy	56
Heddy	60
An Inheritance	67
Living Alone	75
Baseball, Bar Mitzva and Spring	82
Turning Twelve	88
Going on Thirteen	95
Glossary of Hebrew and Yiddish Words	101

I, Jeremy Levi

My name is Jeremiah Levi. That's a long name to have, let me tell you! And how many Jeremiahs did you ever meet? It's not exactly what you'd call a common name, even in Hebrew.

In Hebrew, Jeremiah is pronounced Yirmiyahu, and that's pretty long too. In fact, when I was born, Mom said it was such a long name for such a small baby, that she started calling me Jeremy right away, and that's what mostly everyone calls me now.

In our family, everyone has a Hebrew name. Mom is Miriam, Dad is Gershon, and Zeidy, my Grandpa, is Mattityahu. Daniel and Ezra are my brothers, and Heddy (that's short for Chedva) is my sister.

Even Levi, our family name, is Hebrew. We pronounce it LAY-VEE, just as in Hebrew. The *leviim* used to work in the *Beit Hamikdash* in Jerusalem, and Dad says that when *mashiach* comes and the *Beit Hamikdash* is rebuilt, we'll get our old jobs back. That's one of the reasons I study hard in school. I'd hate to be disqualified from a job in the *Beit Hamikdash* because I didn't learn enough! Although, to tell you the truth, I'm not sure how some of the things we learn in school will help me much. For instance, English grammar. I can't imagine why the *leviim* would have to know English grammar; but Mom says I have to learn it anyway.

I'm eleven, and eleven is a hard age to be, even if your name ISN'T Jeremiah. People expect you to act grown up, but they treat you as if you're a baby just the same. All day long it's "Jeremy come here. Jeremy go there. Jeremy do this. Jeremy stop that!" They never leave you alone.

Take mealtime for example. All I hear is, "Don't slouch. Sit up straight. Did you wash your hands? Take your elbows off the table. Keep your feet still. Stop kicking. Chew your food. Use your knife. Don't forget *birkat hamazon*." What I'd like to know is, how am I supposed to eat and listen to all of those instructions at the same time? It's enough to starve a person to death!

But I shouldn't complain. My family is really O.K. Except for Heddy. She's six. I suppose I could stand her if she weren't my sister, but she is. I wish I didn't have to share a room with her and all her dolls. A boy my age shouldn't have to sleep in a room with dolls. It's embarrassing! All year long I've been begging to sleep in the room with Danny and Ezra, but they say they go to sleep much later than I do and they would keep me up. I wouldn't mind that one bit, really I wouldn't! The truth is, they just don't want me in their room. They think I'm too young. If I had a younger brother, I would be nicer to him!

I'm in the sixth grade in the Kerem HaTorah Yeshiva. I like school, except for the principal, Rabbi Pane. Sometimes he really is a "pain," but I don't usually say so, because if I do, Dad gets angry. Our teacher Rabbi Lang is super, but Rabbi Pane calls me into his office every time I get a low mark and he gives me his speech.

"Yirmiyahu," he says, "what are we going to do with you? You are not fulfilling your potential." (He just loves that word POTENTIAL.) "If you persist in getting marks like 40 and 50 on your examinations, we'll have to reconsider your status in the sixth grade." (He means he'll fail me, but he can't because of all that POTENTIAL of mine. I'm too smart for fifth grade and he knows it.) "Potentially, you are an excellent student. But you must apply yourself! Study! Concentrate! Remember your POTENTIAL!"

Rabbi Lang doesn't get all excited at my marks of 40 and 50. He knows I just don't like tests. It makes me nervous when I have to hurry up and finish before the bell rings.

One day Rabbi Pane called me into his office and waved three tests at me. One was in English grammar of course, and they were all marked 40.

"Well, Yirmiyahu, what do you have to say about this?"

I thought about it for a minute and I couldn't decide between keeping quiet and answering. So then I said in a friendly sort of way, "Aw, it's not SO bad. At least I got forty percent right!"

I guess that was the wrong thing to say because Rabbi Pane's face turned purple and he lowered his voice — a sure sign that he was angry.

"VERY funny! If we were giving out marks for jokes, you would get 100! However, we're not teaching comedy here. You are supposed to be learning. I think the time has come to let you try the fifth grade for a while. Perhaps you'll be more successful at fulfilling your potential there!"

I didn't believe he'd really do it, but he did. He took me into the fifth grade class and announced, "Yirmiyahu is going to be visiting with you for a while."

The kids giggled and Rabbi Stepen looked

embarrassed. I slunk into an empty seat in the last row and didn't open up my mouth the entire day. When I got home, Rabbi Pane had called my mom, and she sent me straight to my room. Then that pesky Heddy (she learns in the girls' school at Kerem) had to go around telling everyone on the block that I was put back in school. I could have strangled her! I was feeling so bad that I didn't even want to see Sammy Travis, and he's my best friend!

The next morning I had an awful headache, but Mom insisted I go to school. She's funny. Sometimes I feel fine and she fusses over me like crazy and takes my temperature and everything, and when I REALLY don't feel well, she sends me to school! I barely managed to crawl out of bed and get dressed. I couldn't even eat breakfast. But when I got to school, was I ever happy. Rabbi Stepen was home sick and we didn't have any substitute. Since I was the oldest kid in the fifth grade, I went up to the front of the room and said, "Listen, if we're quiet and look like we're learning something, Rabbi Pane will leave us alone. But if he thinks we need someone to take care of the class, he's gonna be the one to do it. And we all know what he's like!"

They're a sensible bunch, the fifth graders, I'll

say that for them. They elected me Teacher for the Day, and we got down to business. We *davened shacharit* and then we reviewed the *chumash* from the day before. Next, I showed them an easy short cut for long division that my brother Danny had taught me. They really appreciated that. I don't understand why the teachers don't show us the easy ways to do things and we have to find them out ourselves! When I ran out of teaching ideas, we played some games. Every time Rabbi Pane popped in, we were busy. With a little more practice, I bet I'd make a first rate teacher! When the bell rang, Rabbi Pane came in and said, "Children, I want you to know I appreciate your cooperation today."

Then a little kid in the front row raised his hand and said, "It was all because of Jeremy. He's a great teacher."

Rabbi Pane's face got a little red. For a minute I thought that he was going to get angry again, but instead, he hemmed and hawed, and finally he said, "Well . . . yes. Thank you very much, Yirmiyahu. You're all dismissed now."

The next day he put me back into the sixth grade.

✡ ✡ ✡

The Livyatan and the O.S.C.

As I said, Sammy Travis and I are best friends. ✡

We've been growing up together since we were babies, and we aren't finished yet. Our parents pray in the same synagogue and our mothers went to school together. Sammy and I go to school together too. We've been in the same class since first grade and we always try to sit next to each other. We might even be related because our grandfathers came from the same town in Lithuania and my father said that a lot of the people in the town were relatives. But we're not sure.

Sammy and I have had all sorts of adventures — together, of course. Sometimes we get into trouble together too. Just to give you one example, when we were younger, back in the fourth grade, we used to dream about sailing on a real ship, not just the leaky rowboats in the park lagoon. But we don't live near the ocean, and we didn't have a chance in a million of ever finding a real ship. It was pretty aggravating because we were sure we would have been great sailors!

One day in school, Sammy had a brilliant idea and sent me a note. "It's gonna be YEARS until we get to sail in a real boat. Let's build our own boat meanwhile and get a little practice. I'll meet you in our garage after *mincha*."

There was an old bathtub in Sammy's garage, the kind that has legs on the bottom like claws. Sammy's parents took it out of their bathroom years ago and put in a modern tub. We moved the bathtub into the middle of the garage (Sammy's father usually parks his car out on the street). Then we made a mast out of two broomhandles and we cut up sails from old sheets. We fixed everything up according to the pictures of old schooners we found in a *National Geographic* magazine. We got sewing supplies to fix the sails in case of a storm, a first aid kit, an inner tube for a life preserver, food, and blankets, and all kinds of emergency survival equipment we thought we might need. We were going to ask Rabbi Lang if we had to put a *mezuza* on a boat, until we realized that it didn't have a door.

Mom gave me a broken fan and our shop teacher helped us fix the wiring so that it worked. When everything was all set up, we used to lock the garage door, turn on the fan so that it blew full blast into the sails, and off we went! We'd pretend we were sailing away to all sorts of exciting places.

We took turns deciding where to go, and whoever did the deciding had to bring along the necessary equipment. Once in the summer, Sammy decided to sail to the North Pole and we had to wear winter jackets and boots and scarves. I thought I'd melt! I told him if he did a dumb thing like that again, I'd let him sail alone! He did have a point though. He said it was so hot outside that he thought the North Pole would be a pleasant change!

You can't imagine how lovely it was in that garage. All quiet . . . unless we made the noise. No one to bother us. And the whole world to travel through. Ezra gave us all his old *National Geographic* magazines since we kept borrowing them all the time anyway, and we put them inside the bathtub—I mean the ship! That way we could look up whatever we needed without debarking. My Dad gave us some maps and a compass and Sammy's older sister bought him a real telescope for his birthday. The only trouble was that there was nothing to see on the ceiling of the garage.

We tried drilling a hole in the ceiling so we could see the sky, but Sammy's father heard the drill, and when he came out to see what we were doing, he made us stop. Then we pasted stars on the ceiling to make an indoor sky, like in a planetarium, but they kept falling off. In the end, we gave it up and just moved the ship closer to the window. But even then we never saw any stars because we always played in the daytime.

We did use the telescope one night, though. We asked for permission to sleep in the ship, and we were all ready for our first nocturnal voyage. My brother Ezra said that's what you call nighttime travelling. But to tell the truth, it was a little scary being out in the garage alone, and at around 10 P.M. we decided to go into Sammy's house to sleep. His sister didn't even laugh at us. That's one difference between Sammy's family and mine. Danny and Ezra would have kidded me for weeks about being such a scaredy-cat sailor.

One day Danny asked me what the name of our ship was. I told him it didn't have a name. He said every self-respecting ship has a name. I don't see how a ship is supposed to respect itself, but I figured Danny knew what he was talking about, so I discussed it with Sammy. We looked up names of ships and after a lot of thinking we decided on the *Livyatan*. A *livyatan* is a huge fish, sort of like a whale. In English it's called a leviathan. We

learned all about it in class. It must look very majestic in the water, and we thought our boat would look majestic too — if it had any water to get into. Besides, the name sounded nice. That's when we gave ourselves a name, too — the O.S.C. — the Oceanless Sailors' Club. We chose that because we were the only sailors we knew who didn't have an ocean to sail in.

We kept this up for almost three months, and it was really neat. Even my parents approved of what I was doing for a change. They said I was learning about astronomy and ships, and I was doing my homework in the boat instead of in my bedroom where Heddy always bothered me, so they were happy. They just wanted me to remember to *daven mincha* before I got into the boat after school. But all nice things have to end sometime, and so did this. It was because of Heddy too.

One afternoon my mom had to go to some meeting and there was nowhere to leave Heddy. Heddy was only four then and Mom insisted that she couldn't stay alone, so I had to take her with me when I went to meet Sammy at the *Livyatan*. It was my turn to be captain, and I was planning to sail to *Eretz Yisrael* that day. I had made all sorts of special arrangements, because going to Israel isn't the same as going to other places. It's a special sort of trip.

I hate to babysit for Heddy. I have trouble bossing her around because she's smart enough to answer me back. And if I ever get angry and hit her, even if it's just a small hit, she screams loud enough to burst an eardrum. Then my mother always gets angry at *me*. So it doesn't pay. It's simpler to just give in to her so she'll keep quiet.

Anyway, she got very excited when she saw the boat. For a change, she behaved herself and did whatever we told her, so we thought everything would work out all right. Just as we were about to cast off, she asked, "How come you don't have any water for your boat to sail in? Let's take the hose and fill up the garage floor so it'll be like a real ocean."

At first we started to tell her how dumb that was, but then we thought it over and it didn't seem so dumb at all. It would be kind of nice to have real water to sail in. The fan could blow on the water and make waves. Maybe we could even put in a few fish. The only place the water could seep out from was under the door, so I got some caulking and we sealed it closed. Then I crawled out the window to get the hose and we started filling up the garage. It was taking a long time and I was getting tired, so I lay the hose down on the floor and climbed back into the boat, and we started the trip to Israel.

We had a stormy sea all the way across the Atlantic (we had turned the fan on "high"), but finally, we sailed into the quiet waters of the Mediterranean. As we approached the shores of *Eretz Yisrael,* I felt just as the Rambam or Yehuda HaLevi must have felt when they first made the trip hundreds of years ago. Sammy and I were getting ready to say some *tehillim* as we sighted shore, but just then Heddy started to complain that the trip was taking too long, and she wanted to go home. Well, when Heddy wants something, there's no arguing. She's as stubborn as can be. So we had to turn back at the last minute and the *Livyatan* didn't make it to *Eretz Yisrael* after all.

But by that time, there was a good-sized ocean on the garage floor and we decided to leave it there so we could use it again the next day. We took off our shoes, waded through the water, climbed out the window, and all went home.

Bright and early the next morning, the phone in our house rang. It was Sammy's mother. I could hear her hollering through the receiver even in my room. It seems we forgot to turn off the hose and the water really flooded the place. The garage floor was all moldy and misshapen and the door got pushed open and all that water came tumbling out into Sammy's garden. It washed away half the plants and part of the fence. It flooded up three more yards and the neighbors were having a fit. Worst of all, it flooded our boat and ruined the magazines and the equipment and our fan—the whole works! Even the mast fell down and the sails were all torn and soaked. But nobody cared about *that* except Sammy and me! Adults think only their own things are important! Sammy and I had to clean up the garage and all four yards too. What a mess! I never worked so hard in my life. (Of course no one asked Heddy to help clean up, even though the ocean was all her idea.)

That was the end of the *Livyatan* and the Oceanless Sailors' Club. Danny thought it was all hysterical. Ezra laughed too, but he said one sensible thing. "Even if the boat hadn't been ruined, it would still have been the end of the Oceanless Sailors, because now that you flooded the garage, you aren't oceanless anymore!" Big joke. Only Zeidy understood how I felt.

Now that we're older, we don't do that kind of thing any more, but every time I see a sailor, I still think of the O.S.C., and every time I see a boat, I remember the *Livyatan*.

✡ ✡ ✡
Lashon Hakodesh and Judy's Wedding

✡

In our house, you learn to speak Hebrew. Dad says Hebrew is called *lashon hakodesh*—the Holy Tongue—because the Torah was given in Hebrew and almost all our prayers are in Hebrew. Dad says God understands English too, but it's more fitting for Jews to speak to Him in *lashon hakodesh*.

Last year, Danny and Ezra decided that once a week at supper we should all speak only Hebrew. They said it would be good practice. Every time someone spoke in English, he would be fined ten cents, and the money from the fines would go to *tzedaka*.

In my school, we start learning how to speak Hebrew in the first grade, but there are still a lot of things I don't know how to say. I can pray perfectly well and I know a lot of *chumash,* but it's not so easy to speak a language that's five thousand years old! Especially when you're still in elementary school, like me. By the time that supper was over, I owed two dollars and eighty cents. That's awfully expensive for talking at one meal. Of course, no one fined Heddy, and she spoke English almost the whole time! Ezra admitted that it wasn't such a fair arrangement for me, so he suggested that the following week we should try it again, but this time I wouldn't get fined and everyone should try and use words I know. Ezra is a good guy.

Well, the next week, at the end of the meal, Ezra owed three dollars; Danny owed five dollars and seventy cents (that just shows how much he talks!); Dad owed a dollar sixty; and Mom owed sixty cents (her Hebrew is pretty good). Dad said that at this rate the family would go bankrupt. He paid all the debts himself and said that everyone should brush up on their Hebrew before trying such an expensive experiment again!

But we do speak Hebrew without fines on Friday nights with Zeidy. Zeidy said that in his parents' home, they spoke only Hebrew every *Shabbos*. Even the little children. "On *Shabbos kodesh* we speak *lashon hakodesh*." That's what Zeidy says. And he says we should try not to talk about foolish or bad things in *lashon hakodesh*. A Holy Language should be used for good and important things—like learning Torah. So every Friday night we all learn *parashat hashavua* with Zeidy. It's funny, but when Zeidy speaks to me in

Hebrew, I can understand almost everything he says.

Last year, Sammy and I used to talk Hebrew whenever we were on the bus. It was like talking our own secret language. After a while, we got to be pretty good. If we ever got stuck and didn't know how to say something, we'd use the English word but we'd mix up the syllables so it didn't sound like English.

One day on the way to our dentist appointments (we go to the same dentist), we sat down in the bus across from a fat, funny looking lady. We were talking Hebrew to each other and we started discussing her double chin and her crooked teeth and her funny hat when suddenly, she turned to us and said, "Your Hebrew is awful and your manners are worse!" Later on Zeidy said it's bad enough talking *lashon hara* and gossiping about someone in English, but doing it in Hebrew is terrible! We never did it again.

My family is very interested in *Eretz Yisrael*. The State of Israel is in *Eretz Yisrael* and they talk Hebrew there all the time. My cousin Judy lives there, and you should hear how fast she can speak Hebrew!

Last winter we were invited to Judy's wedding. It was going to be in *Yerushalayim*, the capital of Israel. Was I ever excited! None of my friends had ever been to Israel, so I'd be the first to go. I started making a list of all the places I had to see, places we learned about in school. First of all was *Yerushalayim*. I wanted to walk all around the walls of the Old City and go in all the different gates. And of course I'd go to the *Kotel* to *daven*. Just imagine standing right outside the courtyard of the *Beit Hamikdash*!

Then I'd go to the *Me'arat Hamachpela* in *Chevron*. On the way back I'd stop off in *Beit Lechem* at *Kever Rachel*. Then I'd go up north to the *Galil* and down south to the *Negev*. And then I'd go . . . well, I'd just go EVERYWHERE!

I told my friends about the trip, and the first thing you know, they started planning a goodbye party for me. Meanwhile, I thought I'd better improve my Hebrew and I asked Mom for a Hebrew-English pocket dictionary. I walked around memorizing words and I must have learned at least a hundred new ones a week. In fact, I was doing so well that after two weeks, Rabbi Pane called me into his office to say, "Yirmiyahu, your Hebrew has improved amazingly lately. This is what happens when you live up to your POTENTIAL!"

When Mom and Dad went to take pictures for

their passports and they took Heddy along, but not me, I became a little worried. That night I asked Mom when I was going to take *my* passport pictures. She looked up from the book she was reading and seemed a little surprised.

"But Jeremy dear, what do you need a passport for?"

As soon as she said that, a warning signal started buzzing in my head. I answered as calmly as I could, "To go to Judy's wedding of course."

Mom got this odd expression on her face. "But dear, no one said anything about YOU going to Judy's wedding."

"But we ARE going, aren't we? We go to ALL the family weddings, don't we?"

"Of course we'll go," says my mother. "That is, Dad and I will go, and we're thinking of taking Heddy along because she's too young to stay here without us. But we can't ALL go. It's much too expensive!"

I know I'm eleven, and eleven-year-olds aren't supposed to cry. Not much anyhow. But somehow, all these tears got into my eyes and all I could say was, "Heddy? You want to take Heddy and leave me here? That's not fair!"

I ran to my room. Heddy was in there playing some stupid game with her friends. I chased them out and slammed the door shut. I could hear her running and crying to Mom, but I didn't care. I threw myself down on the bed, shoes and all, and concentrated on feeling miserable. I was very successful too. I don't think I ever felt so perfectly miserable before, not even on the day they put me back to the fifth grade.

I thought of running away, just to scare my parents, but I couldn't think of any place to run to. Then I thought of going to Judy's wedding myself. Wouldn't they be surprised if I showed up by myself in *Yerushalayim*! I could take a bus to New York and stow away on a ship or a plane going to Israel. At first it sounded a little silly, even to me, but then I remembered reading a story in the paper about a boy who wanted to go back to Puerto Rico when his parents moved to New York. He hid in a big freighter and got halfway there before they found him. Then it was too late to turn back, so he really did get to Puerto Rico, even though he didn't stay there long.

I'd have to borrow Danny's duffle bag if I went. He'd be angry that I took it without asking, but I'd return it as soon as I got back. I'd tell Sammy I was going so he wouldn't worry, but I wouldn't even leave my parents a note. I didn't care if they worried their heads off! Besides that, they'd be so busy taking Heddy to Israel that they probably wouldn't even miss me.

I was thinking so hard that I didn't hear my dad come in (he walks pretty quietly for an adult). He said, "Can I sit down, Jeremy?"

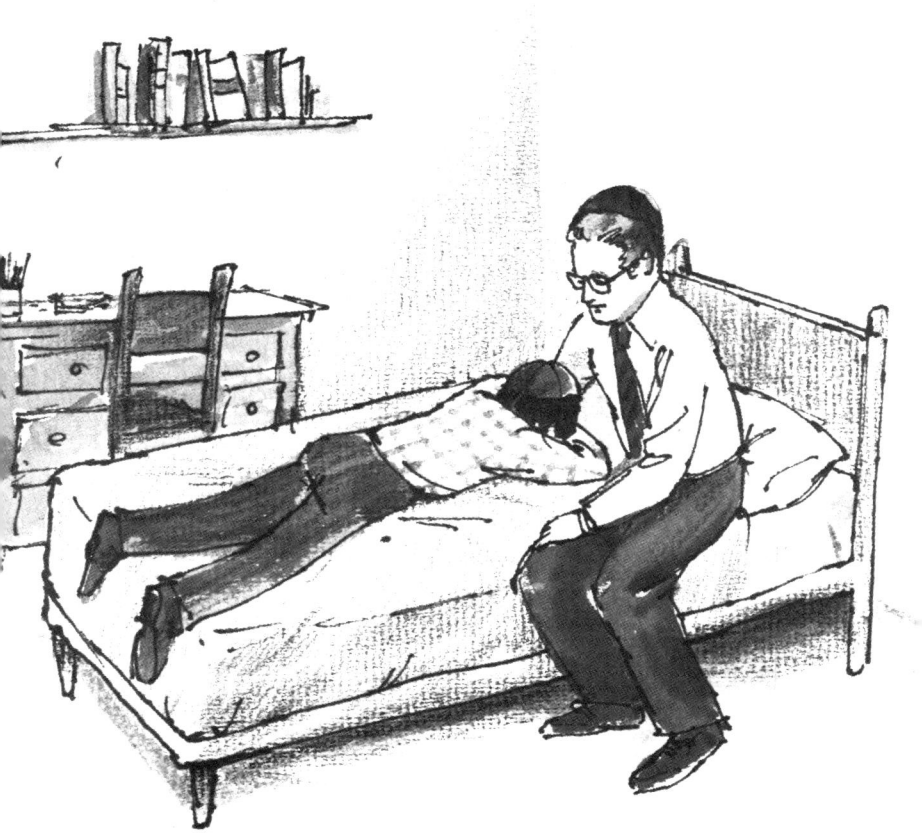

I didn't answer him, but he sat down anyway. He started explaining how much money it cost for each airplane ticket and how he couldn't afford to take the whole family. He said he knew Heddy was often "difficult" and that's why they didn't want to leave her with me and Danny and Ezra. He said he and Mom thought that I was pretty grown up now and that I could stay alone with my two older brothers and manage nicely. But if I really wanted to go, he'd stay home and I could go in his place!

My first reaction was, "Great! I accept!" But then I felt a little bad. Mom and Dad hadn't had a vacation in a long time. I was at Yeshiva Camp last summer, but they didn't go anywhere because Heddy was sick with the mumps and the flu all summer long. And they hadn't ever been to *Eretz Yisrael* yet either. I knew they were both very excited about going. I also wasn't sure how much I liked the idea of going alone with just Mom and Heddy. It meant that I would get stuck taking care of Heddy all the time.

I told Dad I'd have to think about it. The next day I had a long discussion about all the pros and cons of the matter with Zeidy. It wasn't easy, but in the end, I told the kids to cancel my going-away party and I decided to stay home.

It wasn't so bad either! The kids made me the

party anyway; they said they didn't want to waste all the things they bought. And I had the bedroom all to myself for two whole weeks. Danny and Ezra were really swell to me and I stayed up late with them every night. The best part was that everyone treated me like a hero. They kept telling me what a nice thing I did—giving up a trip to Israel so that my father could go. And do you know what? After a while, I wasn't even sorry anymore. In fact, I was glad I stayed home!

It's just too bad that Heddy managed to spoil Mom and Dad's vacation again. This time, she got the measles and she was sick in bed at Judy's house straight through the wedding!

✡ ✡ ✡
The Klezmerim
✡

In Hebrew, *kley zemer* means musical instruments. In Yiddish, *klezmerim* are musicians. That's because musicians play instruments and Yiddish has a whole bunch of Hebrew mixed in. (I figured I'd better tell you that right now or you might not understand what this chapter is all about!)

Zeidy says we're a bunch of *klezmerim* in our house, because we make so much music. Everybody plays something. Mom plays the piano and Dad plays the violin. Danny learned clarinet and Ezra has a flute. The best of all is Zeidy himself. He plays the harmonica. Sometimes they all play together and it sounds pretty good. We have a big family with lots of cousins and aunts and uncles, and whenever they all get together, Dad gets our orchestra going.

I don't know who did the deciding, but I got slotted to play the piano like Mom. No one asked for my opinion in the matter or I would have told them that what I really wanted was to learn how to play the drums. When I brought the subject up, Mom said that we already had a piano in the house and buying drums would cost too much money. I suggested that we could sell the piano and use the money to buy me drums, but Mom said drums were too noisy. So it was decided that I would start piano lessons. Sometimes I wonder why they teach us all this stuff about democracy when no one practices it very much. Not in my family anyway.

I started piano lessons, but I arranged to play the drums on the side. Sammy and I got these gigantic empty cans from the school lunchroom. We asked the cook to save them for us. Each size made a different sound. We experimented a little and tried wrapping them up with different materials to mute the banging. It was pretty neat. If we wrapped a can up with newspaper, it sounded one way. If we put a wool blanket around it, it sounded completely different. We stuffed some of the cans and made holes in others. We had about twenty different sizes. We painted them different colors and set them up with wires in a semicircle so I could sit in the middle and reach them all. Sammy was great. He went to all this trouble just to help me. He couldn't play himself because he doesn't have any sense of rhythm.

When the drums were all set up, we began thinking about starting a band. Sammy was especially keen about it because I told him he could be the business manager. He got a kid from seventh grade who played the guitar and my cousin Moish agreed to play his xylophone with us. We would have liked Danny's clarinet, but if Danny came in, he'd take the whole band over and we wanted to manage it ourselves, so we didn't ask him. Yossi down the block heard about us and said he could play the tuba, but we'd have to help him carry it to wherever we practiced and then back to his house. It was exciting to have a real tuba. It gave us a very professional look. Another cousin of mine wanted to join with his violin, but Sammy pointed out to him that no one could hear a violin with all of the noisy instruments we had, so he stayed out. I wanted Zeidy to play his harmonica solo, but he said he was too old for such lively music. He prefers quieter songs himself.

Our next problem was finding a place to practice. You wouldn't believe how uncooperative adults are. They're always lecturing how important a musical education is, but they don't do a thing to help, unless you're getting educated THEIR way! In short, we couldn't find a place until Mr. Spitzer, the janitor from the school, got permission for us to play in the gym after school. He promised Rabbi Pane that he'd be responsible for the building and for us. Danny said the janitor didn't mind because he was very hard of hearing and our noise wouldn't bother him, but it's not true. Mr. Spitzer told us he appreciated fine music and he thought we had a great future ahead of us!

The first song we learned was *Hiney ma tov uma na'im*. Each of us learned the notes at home, but then we discovered that it was easier playing alone than playing together! While the xylophone was on *hiney ma tov*, the tuba was on *uma na'im* and the guitar was strumming way ahead at *shevet achim* and I (the drums, in case you've forgotten) had already reached *gam yachad*! It was obvious that we needed a conductor. We tried using Sammy, but as I said before, he has absolutely no sense of rhythm. Then we tried Mr. Spitzer, but I must admit that Danny might have been right. I don't think he heard us at all. He just hummed to himself and waved his hands around and confused things even more.

I discussed the problem with Mom. She knows a lot about music. She smiled this funny-looking smile she gets every so often and said, "I know JUST the person for you. He's always wanted to be a conductor." I couldn't see what was so funny, but then again my mom is always laughing at things I don't think are funny. However, this time her idea really WAS funny. She asked my dad! When I thought of my father standing in front of our band with my twenty painted drums, even I laughed! Danny and Ezra thought it was pretty funny too. But Dad didn't. He thought it was a wonderful idea. I'll never understand adults!

Dad came down to the gym, and he did a good job, I must admit. He was a real sport, too, and nobody minded that he was my dad. He really helped straighten us out, so well in fact, that after a few weeks, we could even play together when he wasn't there. The thing that still confuses me is how come he couldn't stand the noise when I played the drums all alone at home, but when I played with three other noisy instruments in the gym where the echo was deafening, he didn't mind at all! As I said, I'll never understand adults.

We played all Hebrew songs and we called ourselves *The Klezmerim*. Zeidy said that when the *klezmerim* played at weddings in the Jewish towns in Europe, their music brought real *simcha* to everyone and made everyone happy. We wanted our music to bring *simcha* to people too, so we practiced a lot. Eventually, we got so good that Rabbi Pane asked us to play for a school assembly.

Then we entered a contest for school bands. We won second prize, and they asked us to play on the radio, although that didn't work out too well because of the microphones. Normally, we don't use a microphone. We don't need one because we play loud. But we forgot to tell them that at the radio station, so it was a little ear-shattering until their technicians adjusted the instruments down to lo *N*-low.

But the best performance we ever gave was at the Old Age Home on Purim. We strummed and blew and pounded away for three hours while everyone sang and danced. Our music really did bring *simcha* to those people, and they didn't even mind the noise. They paid us eighteen dollars for the afternoon, but we gave the money back to the Home as a donation.

Our band stayed together until Mr. Spitzer got sick. His replacement was cleaning out the gym one day and he found my drums. Anyone with a little intelligence could see that they were drums, but he thought they were cans, and he threw them away. Before we could retrieve them, the garbage men collected the garbage, and that was the end of the drum collection. Then our tuba player moved to a different city, and my father didn't have time to conduct anymore. We were getting a little tired of the band anyway, so we didn't mind too much. Except for Sammy. He had set up an office in his bedroom and he even convinced his father to let him have his own extension phone, just like a real manager. But after the band fell apart, he didn't have any more business and he took it kind of hard. So I promised him I'd try and come up with something new for him. After all, what are friends for if not to help each other out?

✡✡✡
The J&S Employment Agency
✡

Every day in school Sammy would come up to ask me if I had any ideas yet for a business for him. I didn't think of anything until one night when Mom asked me to do the dishes after supper.

"How come you never ask Danny or Ezra? Or Heddy? She's big enough to help."

"Danny and Ezra aren't here," said Mom. "You know they don't come home from the yeshiva until 7:30."

"Well, it's not fair that I get stuck with the dishes every night. Can't you hire someone to do them?"

"Find me someone to hire and I'll hire him. Until then, would you please do the dishes?"

Mom makes it sound as if she were asking a question, but it's no question at all. She wasn't *asking* if I would do the dishes. She was *saying*, "Do the dishes!" But she gave me an idea. I bet there are lots of parents with lots of jobs and I bet they'd be happy to pay someone to do them. And there are plenty of kids around who would be willing to work! This was just the kind of thing Sammy would be interested in hearing about.

I finished the dishes in ten minutes (sometimes it can take me an hour if I'm not in any particular hurry) and I went to Sammy's house. Before I'd even finished telling him what I had in mind, he understood. He's a pretty bright guy. (That's why he always has so much spare time for projects like this. He finishes his homework in half the time it takes everybody else.) We didn't waste any time. We sat right down and wrote two advertisements.

> WANTED!
> Responsible students from the 5th
> to the 8th grades interested in
> doing jobs around the neighborhood.
> Work your own hours. Fair pay.
> J & S EMPLOYMENT AGENCY
> (call 842-3791 after school)

The *J* in J & S Employment Agency was myself, Jeremy. The *S* was Sammy. The telephone number was Sammy's too. His extension phone was back in business!

We put that sign up on the schoolyard gate.

Then we made a second sign. It said:

> Do you need help?
> THE J & S EMPLOYMENT AGENCY
> can supply you with someone to:
> clean, mow & water your lawn
> walk your dog
> care for your pets
> do home deliveries
> babysit
> clean your garage, attic or basement.
> Our prices are fair.
> Our work guaranteed satisfactory.
> Call the J & S Employment Agency
> after school is out. 842-3791

We put this sign up all around the neighborhood and we were swamped! Sammy's extension phone didn't stop ringing. It seemed as if every kid in the fifth, sixth, seventh, and eighth grades had some free time and wanted to work, and every family in the neighborhood needed something.

Zeidy asked if we'd be willing to help some of his elderly friends who couldn't pay us. For instance, Mr. Linker needed someone to take him down to the doctor every Wednesday afternoon. Sammy and I said sure, we'd help them too, and we decided to change our name to the J & S EMPLOYMENT AND MITZVA AGENCY.

Things got so busy that we had to hire Sammy's younger sister Rachel to answer the phone and take messages. When someone came in for work, we took his name and telephone number, and when someone called up to have a job done, we'd figure out a fair price and send a kid over to do the job. The Agency got five percent of the price of each job done, unless it was one of our *gemillat chesed* cases. Then we did it for free.

After three weeks, you could see the difference in the neighborhood. The lawns all looked much neater and nicer. Parents were in better spirits, because with all the available babysitting, they were getting out a lot more. The stores were happy to have us delivering for them. They said that their customers were buying more now that we were delivering merchandise. We had about seventy-five kids working for us. Everyone was making money or getting some service and the kids were all giving *tzedaka* from the money they earned. Sammy's phone rang continuously. It was a very successful organization. The only drawback was the kids. Between school and their jobs, they were getting a little tired.

Then the P.T.A. met. That was the beginning of the end. Adults are SO unreasonable at times. Instead of all the nagging they had been doing to get their kids to help, here we were arranging for OTHER kids to do their work for them, and with a smile too. Instead of having to hand out allowances and money all the time and complaining how we should earn our own money so we'll appreciate its value, here we all were earning our own money—lots of it. But do you think they were satisfied? No sir!

They all went to this P.T.A. meeting, and the first thing on the agenda was "Why is Kerem Yeshiva encouraging its pupils to work without their parents' permission?" Rabbi Pane got up, all red in the face, and said the school had nothing to do with it. Why were the parents allowing their children to work three to four hours a day after school, so that everyone showed up dead tired every morning? Everyone got all excited, and they all forgot that EVERY SINGLE ONE OF THEM had hired someone from the Agency at one time or another.

The next thing you know, my father has this brilliant realization that, "As a result of this employment agency, we're no longer able to ask our own children to do anything for us, because they're always busy working for someone else. In effect, we are now being forced to 'hire' someone else's child while our own is busy working for our neighbor!"

Of course, when you put it that way, it doesn't sound so good. Sammy's parents complained loudest of all. They said their phone bill had tripled and they could never get on the line. So they all mulled over the subject a little and then they took a vote and decided unanimously that each parent would tell his child that he could no longer work for us. I ask you, does that sound fair?

Only Rabbi Lang remembered to mention that we weren't only an employment agency. We were a *mitzva* firm too! We did a lot of *gemillat chesed* and helped people in all sorts of ways. We were doing all the things we learned about in school.

But it didn't make any difference. They voted against us anyway, and I'm very happy to report that after two weeks, they were all sorry! All the kids were back asking their folks for money, and all the parents were back nagging their kids to help in the house. That just goes to show you how unreasonable parents can be!

Mom tried hard to explain to me why we should be willing to help in our own homes without being paid. She said we were all big kids, and as part of a family, it was our responsibility to help out. I told her that as soon as I saw Heddy helping (I admit that Danny and Ezra help a lot when they're home, but they're usually gone!), I'd buckle down and help too. Mom said Heddy is younger than I am. I said that if she wanted Heddy to turn out better than I did, she should start training her now. We didn't convince each other, and the end of the story was that I was right back at the beginning . . . at the sink, washing the supper dishes.

✡✡✡
Running the House
✡

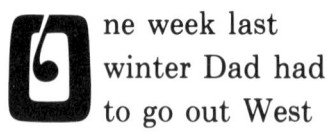

One week last winter Dad had to go out West on business. I begged to go with him, but he told me, "You're too young to come travelling with me when I'm on business. Maybe I'll take you along sometime next year."

Then I asked if I could finally get my own bedroom, or at least not have to share a room with Heddy anymore, but Mom and Dad both said, "You're not old enough to need a room of your own yet. You'll get one when you're a little older."

And when I wanted to go to Sammy's house one night during the week, I was told, "You're too young to go out on school nights."

Whenever I want something, I'm too young, or too little, or else I'm not old enough. But at the same time, they're always telling me, "Why don't you act your age? When are you going to grow up? Why are you such a baby?" I wish they'd make up their minds already, so I'd know how to act!

Anyway, while Dad was away, Ezra came

down with double pneumonia and the doctor said he had to go to the hospital immediately. Mom went with him and stayed in the hospital for five days! Danny was in the middle of studying for a big *gemara* exam, and he was so nervous that you couldn't even talk to him. Zeidy would have come to stay with us, but he was out of town visiting his sister.

I asked Mom, "What are we supposed to do alone? Danny says he doesn't even have time to go to the grocery store." Mom told me, "You're a big boy, Jeremy, and I have to depend on you. I just can't think of anything but Ezra right now. You'll have to be responsible for the house. I know you can manage."

The first thing I did was attend to Heddy. "Listen, Heddy," I told her, "Mom says I have to take care of things around here until Ezra gets out of the hospital. I'm making you my assistant. You have to do everything I tell you. Most of all, you have to LISTEN to me. Otherwise, I will not be responsible for the consequences."

She wasn't sure what that meant, but it didn't sound friendly, and even though Heddy is young, she's not stupid. She knew that Mom and Dad wouldn't be around, so she couldn't go complaining to them. Danny wouldn't listen to her either. So she settled down to being my assistant. She's a pretty good worker when she feels like working, and we did a super cleaning job. We dusted and polished all the furniture. Then I put a load of laundry in the washing machine. We went to the Koshermart and bought hot dogs and chili for supper. Heddy thought we should buy something more nutritious, so she threw two packages of frozen cauliflower into the wagon. Neither of us eats cauliflower, so I didn't see how it was going to improve our diet any, but I let her have her way.

We enjoyed our supper (except that she should have cooked the hot dogs a little longer; they were kind of raw). And we drank a lot of soda and juice after the chili. Then we said *birkat hamazon* and cleaned up, and I let her stay up in bed and read. I figured this was one night we could stay up as long as we liked. After all, I was running the house and there was no one to tell me to go to bed (Danny was studying at a friend's house). But Heddy got tired and went to sleep and I got bored sitting in the den all by myself. I was tired too, after all the work we put in. So I went to sleep half an hour later.

All in all, the first day turned out fine. The only hitch was the oily spot on the rug in Mom's bedroom. When I was polishing the furniture, the bottle of polish spilled and made this big spot on the rug. We couldn't get it out, so I put a small throw rug on top of it. I'm sure Mom will understand and not get upset. At least I hope so.

As I said, Mom didn't come home for five days. Ezra was pretty sick. We couldn't even visit him because he was contagious. But we said *tehillim* for him every day. When I told Rabbi Lang how sick he was, he had the whole class say *tehillim* every day after *mincha*. Later on, Ezra told me he was sure our *tehillim* helped him even more than the penicillin he took!

On the third day of Ezra's stay in the hospital, Dad came home. When he saw what a good job I was doing of running things, he said I should keep the job until Mom came back. He just asked that Heddy cook something besides hot dogs and chili for supper. He said his stomach wasn't as young as it used to be.

Heddy remembered the cauliflower and offered to cook that instead, but when she looked for it in the freezer, it wasn't there. We found it in the food cabinet. I guess we stuck it in there by mistake, and now it was all soggy and moldy and spoiled. So she made Dad a tomato and lettuce sandwich instead.

Finally, Ezra got better. The doctor said there was no danger anymore and Mom could go home. But when she came back, she looked so tired that Heddy and I offered to take care of the house for another day, to give her a chance to rest. It's too bad I threw my navy blue sweatshirt in the laundry together with Mom's good white towels, but I didn't know it would dye everything blue. I just wanted to help a little more by doing the laundry. Mom was a little upset, but she didn't say anything.

In fact, she and Dad really appreciated everything we did for them. When Ezra came home and

Danny had passed his test, Dad bought everybody presents. I got a Dictionary of the Talmud. It was real neat. Now I could look up all the hard words I didn't know without having to ask Ezra or Danny. Whenever I had needed to know something, Ezra had always said, "I'll look it up for you in a few minutes." Then he'd forget. And Danny always said, "Ask Dad. I don't have time now."

The nicest thing was Dad's speech. He told the whole family (Zeidy was there too) what a wonderful job I'd done, and how grown up and responsible I was, and how I had saved the week.

I figured this was an ideal time to ask for my own bedroom. They couldn't tell me I was still too young after having just told me how grown up I was! So I asked.

"Well," said Mom, "that's a problem. Danny and Ezra's room is too small for three beds. And we don't have another room to spare. Wait a little while longer, Jeremy. When Danny goes out of town to yeshiva next year, you can share the room with Ezra."

You think that sounds reasonable? Well, it isn't! What it means is that Heddy will then have a room all to herself while I'll be sharing a room with someone else! Life just isn't fair!

✡ ✡ ✡
Zeidy

Zeidy says I'm wrong about life. He says life may not always *seem* fair, but looks can be deceiving. He says that everything that happens is planned by *Hashem,* so it's fair and wise although we don't always understand it. That's why we say *gam zu letova* even for things we think are bad.

Instead of worrying about my own room so much, Zeidy thinks I should make the best of things and try to see the bright side of the coin. He slept in one room with four brothers and sisters and he says they managed just fine. It's funny, but if someone else told me that, I'd feel annoyed at all their advice, but when Zeidy says it, I don't mind at all.

No one minds when Zeidy tells them things. That's because Zeidy is an unusual man. His father, Yirmiyahu (I'm named after him), lived in Shirvint, a small town in Lithuania. He was a rich man. He owned a lumberyard. When both he and his wife died, Zeidy decided to come to America.

He brought a big fat packet of Russian rubles with him — his inheritance from his father. It was worth a lot of money in those days. But then they had a big revolution in Russia and the new government printed different money, so Zeidy's rubles weren't worth anything at all. They were just a lot of gold and pink colored paper.

But Zeidy didn't complain. He became a carpenter. He chose carpentry because he always loved the smell of freshly cut wood in his father's lumberyard. He learned how to make beautiful furniture and cabinets, and after a while, he had a business of his own. All the new immigrants wanted to work for him because his shop was closed on Shabbos. In those days, stores were open six days a week and it was hard to find a job where you could keep Shabbos. But Zeidy's employees could. They even had a *minyan* in the shop three times a day!

Now that Zeidy is retired, he learns Torah most of the time, but even when he was working he sat and studied every single night. He says the only two nights he missed since his *bar mitzva* were his wedding night and the night my mother was born! When my grandmother died a few years ago, Zeidy said he was going to move to *Eretz Yisrael,* but Mom was so unhappy that he promised to wait until I'm *bar mitzva*. I don't think I could be *bar mitzva* if Zeidy weren't here. He's going to teach me to read in the Torah. Dad or Danny or Ezra could do it, but Zeidy has a special tune and I want to learn his way. It's the way they sang it in Shirvint.

I'm really lucky to have a Zeidy like mine. You should see the *sukka* he built for us. He cut and sanded and stained all the parts by himself, and they all fit together without a single nail or screw!

Zeidy bakes too. Every week he makes a batch of oatmeal cookies. When I eat breakfast at his house on Monday and Thursday mornings after *shul*, he gives me a glass of milk and his oatmeal cookies, but *he* drinks a tiny glass of *shnapps*. I tasted it once, and it was awful!

But the best things about Zeidy are his listening and his explaining. He always has time to listen to me when everyone else is busy, and he explains things so that you really understand them. I wish he could be my teacher in school but he says he's too old to teach. I don't see why. It seems to me that the older you get, the more you've learned. And the more you've learned, the more you could teach!

Zeidy has a new *tallit* but he doesn't put it on

to *daven*; he keeps it folded up in his drawer. Mom keeps asking him to take it out and wear it, but he says he's saving it. He calls it his "*mashiach tallit.*" He's the only person I know who is saving something new to wear for when *mashiach* comes.

Once, I decided to put a new sweater away and save it for *mashiach* too, but Mom said I was growing right out of it and I had better start wearing it quick. (That's one good thing about being grown up; your clothes don't get small!)

I'm really going to miss Zeidy when he moves to *Eretz Yisrael.* Maybe by then I can go with him and learn in a yeshiva there. My Hebrew is pretty good by now. Come to think of it, that's a great way to get away from Heddy!

✮ ✮ ✮
Heddy

As I told you,
Heddy is six.
The trouble with her
is that she acts like she's three but she thinks like she's thirteen! It always amazes me how someone can be so smart and act like such a baby. My mom says I was no different, but I don't believe it.

Heddy taught herself how to read while she was in kindergarten, so when she went into first grade there was nothing for her to do. They had to put her up to the second grade. But the kids there were too old for her. So they kept putting her back and forth for a while, trying to see where she fit in best. The poor kid felt like a yoyo. That's what comes of being too smart for your age, although I suppose it's not her fault. She can't help it if she's smart. She was just born that way.

Heddy always asks me questions. She must think I'm a walking encyclopedia. I wouldn't mind if she'd ask NORMAL questions that I could answer. I wouldn't even mind if I had to look up the answers for her. But she asks such complicated things! The weirdest ideas float around in her head. She wants to know why the moon doesn't fall down onto the earth, and how did the baby trees get into the seeds so that they can grow, and what makes water feel wet, and if she can READ backwards, why can't she THINK backwards? How am I supposed to answer questions like that? It annoys me when she asks me things I can't answer. I usually tell her she's asking stupid questions. Then she tells me I'M stupid because I can't answer. The thing that bothers me is that she might be right!

Mom says that Heddy is actually paying me a big compliment by asking me all these questions. It means that she thinks I'm pretty smart. But how can she think I'm smart, when most of the time, I can't answer her?

Mom says I should try to be nicer to Heddy and maybe I'd even get to enjoy her company more. Actually, the *less* I have of Heddy's company, the *more* I like her! Mom said that if I want Danny and Ezra to act nice to me, I should act nice to Heddy too. I didn't think it would help any, but I agreed to try.

Heddy was always asking for a pet so I thought I'd buy her one. There was a gorgeous monkey in the pet shop, but it cost two hundred dollars, and I wasn't sure my folks would like it. Besides, I only had two dollars saved up just then. So I settled for a real neat little turtle that cost fifty cents. Turtle food cost me $1.29. That left me twenty-one cents for an ice cream cone.

I asked Mom for a dish for the turtle, and I fixed up an island with sand and gravel. I put water in the dish and the turtle had a good home. I wanted to surprise Heddy with it before she went to sleep, so I left it on her pillow, but that didn't turn out to be such a good idea. She ran into the room and sat down on the bed without looking and the whole thing spilled over. We had to change all the linen and Mom was annoyed. That's what comes of trying to be nice to Heddy!

But she really liked that turtle. You couldn't get her away from it. She named him Kolonymus (don't ask me why; it was just another of her crazy ideas!) and she fed him around five times a day. She was always changing his water and exercising him. Finally, I told her she'd exhaust him to death if she didn't leave him alone for a while! It's a good thing she was away at school for a few hours a day, so the poor thing could rest!

One Friday afternoon when I came into the house, Heddy was hysterical. It seems she got this idea that the turtle needed a bath for *Shabbos*.

She filled up the bathroom sink and put detergent into the water, and she literally scrubbed him to death! She wasn't satisfied just washing his shell. Maybe he would have survived that. But Heddy was determined to do a thorough job. She made it her business to pull out his feet and his head and wash them too! Shortly after his bath, poor Kolonymus died.

I arranged the burial ceremony out in the yard, and I assured Heddy that the turtle didn't think she was a murderer (although I had a few doubts on that score myself). I told her he didn't think anything at all, especially now that he was dead. It was just an unfortunate accident and she should try not to worry about it.

But she did though. For a couple of weeks she kept having nightmares about turtles, and she woke me up so often that Mom finally let me sleep in the living room until she calmed down. All of this just goes to show you how silly someone smart can be!

But Heddy really is smart. There's no getting away from it. Sammy and I were reading this book of spy stories, and we thought that it would be fun if we had a secret code of our own now that we weren't talking Hebrew on the bus anymore. It took us around five hours to make up a code. It was pretty complicated too. We started sending each other notes and letters and we left messages all over the place.

Danny saw some of them and he was curious. He asked me to decode one for him, but I said, "No way!" He tried to figure it out, but then he said it wasn't worth his time. Of course what he REALLY meant was that he couldn't do it!

Two days later, in walked Heddy. She was holding one of Sammy's notes as she proudly announced, "At 4 o'clock. I told him."

"What are you talking about?" I asked her.

"Sammy wants to know when you're going for your haircut, so I told him," she answered.

"How do you know he wants to know when I'm going for my haircut?" I asked.

"Because he wrote it here. See?" and she showed me the note. Well, I almost fell flat on my face!

I started hollering, "Who showed you how to read that?"

She started crying and hollered back, "I figured it out myself!" I didn't believe her until she sat down and explained to me exactly how she did it.

Danny and Ezra were floored. They kept telling her how smart she was. Dad too. Then, when they'd all convinced her she was a budding genius, she started telling all her friends how she broke her big brother's code and how easy it was. I didn't mind their thinking she was smart, but they all thought that Sammy and I were pretty dumb to invent a code that was easy enough for Heddy to understand! They didn't know that even Danny couldn't read it! The whole thing was very embarrassing. Sammy said he wasn't going to be friends with me anymore if I couldn't get rid of Heddy, but what did he expect me to do, make her disappear? My mother wouldn't have appreciated that!

All in all, I felt pretty miserable. The only one who sympathized with me a little was Mom. She kept saying, "Wait a little while, Jeremy. Everything will get easier, you'll see. Heddy will grow up and act older and she won't bother with you and your friends so much. And you really will get your own room."

I butted in right then and there and said, "WHEN?" but Mom only said, "Eventually. It won't take so long. You'll see. Soon you'll be twelve and then it will only be a year until your *bar mitzva*. Before you know it, you'll be in high school! You won't stay eleven forever!"

I suppose she's right. After all, she was eleven once too, and now she's a mother. But it seems to me that it's taking an awfully long time. Sometimes I wonder how I'm going to survive until I grow up!

✡✡✡
An Inheritance
✡

Brian Kohn is a boy who lives down the block. He doesn't go to the Kerem Yeshiva, but we're on the neighborhood baseball team together. Brian's family doesn't keep too many *mitzvot*. I guess they never learned very much about being Jewish. I invited Brian over to our house a couple of times, but then, when he invited me back, his mother kept offering me things to eat. I told her I was sorry but I couldn't eat in their house because we only eat kosher food.

Brian wanted to know more about keeping kosher, so I had Zeidy explain it all to him. I don't think Brian's kitchen is kosher yet, but now Brian buys his candy and stuff at the Koshermart so that he can offer me some. Brian is a good friend and I like him. I wish he'd transfer to Kerem Yeshiva. It's too bad he's missing out on so much. He doesn't even know how to read Hebrew.

Anyway, Brian was in the hospital with a broken leg, and I thought I should go visit him. I brought him some books and my favorite game and some cupcakes my mom baked. I told him he was giving me a chance to perform the *mitzva* of *bikkur cholim*, of visiting the sick. Around five o'clock I said goodbye and went out into the hall.

As I was walking towards the elevator, I remembered that Mom said Mrs. Kirshen, an old lady who *davens* in our *shul*, was also in the hospital and it would be nice if I stopped by to say hello to her. I didn't have anything to talk to Mrs. Kirshen about, but I remember that when we were little, she would always give us candy when she saw us. This was a good chance to do something nice for her in return, so I asked the nurse which room she was in.

Brian was in the children's ward on the third floor. It was decorated and full of pictures, and there were a lot of games. But Mrs. Kirshen was in a ward for elderly people who really looked very sick. I was changing my mind about going in to visit when I found myself standing in front of an open door looking right at her!

At first, she seemed surprised to see me, but then she smiled and said, "Hello, Jeremy. What are you doing here?"

I couldn't very well walk away, so I said I had come to visit her.

"To visit? Did you come here to visit me? Your mother is a kind woman, Jeremy, a really kind woman! And it's very nice of you to bother with an old lady."

For a minute I couldn't understand what my mother had to do with it, but then I realized that she thought my mother had sent me to see her. Come to think of it, that WAS the reason I was there! I took off my jacket again and sat down on a chair near her bed and racked my brain for something to say. All I could think of was "How do you feel?" which was pretty dumb, because if she felt well, she wouldn't be in the hospital!

She said, "*Baruch Hashem*, I'm coming along nicely."

The only other thing I could think of was "Does your family come to see you?" I know that if I were in the hospital, my parents and brothers and Zeidy and my aunts and uncles and cousins, even Heddy, would be visiting me all the time. The only reason we didn't visit Ezra when he was in the hospital was that he was contagious.

Mrs. Kirshen started telling me that her two sons lived far away in California. Her husband and her brothers and sisters and most of her friends had died. She had some nieces and nephews, but they lived in different cities and she didn't see them much. She said Rabbi Michlen from our *shul* came to see her every few days and my mom came twice a week, but that was all.

I thought to myself that it must be awfully sad to be all alone and only have a rabbi and someone's mother to visit you if you were sick. Mrs. Kirshen asked me about Heddy and Danny and Ezra. I said everybody was fine, and then, just to have something to talk about, I started telling her about Heddy and the turtle. Then I got started on what a pest Heddy could be, and what an unhelpful brother Danny was sometimes. Ezra was better, but he was usually too busy to spend much time with me. I really didn't mean to tell tales about my family, but it seemed important to talk about SOMETHING and I couldn't think of anything else.

Well, Mrs. Kirshen started talking about when SHE was a young girl. It was hard to imagine wrinkled Mrs. Kirshen ever being a girl, but I guess she was . . . once. She had nine sisters and brothers, and her father was a rabbi in Poland. She told me how they all helped her mother bake *challa* for the whole town every Thursday (it was a pretty small town) and how they brought the *challot* to everyone on Friday mornings in a wheelbarrow!

Every winter they were practically all snowed in—ten kids in a three room house! I'd go crazy if I had to stay in the house with Heddy all winter long, even if I had a room to myself!

Before I knew it, it was 7:30. "I have to go now, Mrs. Kirshen. My mom is going to be angry at me for missing supper and coming home so late. But I really liked talking to you. I never knew so many interesting things happened in Poland! Maybe you can tell me some more if I come back again."

Mrs. Kirshen looked so happy when I said that, that I felt funny. I guess she was pretty lonesome.

When I came home and told Mom what happened, she didn't say a word about missing supper. She just said, "If you told her you're coming back, Jeremy, be sure and remember. Otherwise she'll be terribly disappointed."

To make a long story short, I visited Mrs. Kirshen three times in the hospital. Then I would stop off at her house for a few minutes every day on my way home from school. Some of the kids laughed at me and said I was turning into a regular old woman, but I didn't care. I really liked Mrs. Kirshen, and she really liked my coming.

One day she asked me if I would like to see

some of her 'treasures.' I said, "Sure I would." She opened up an old trunk she kept in her bedroom and pulled out the drawers. Each one had something in it. Coins from all over the world; some old jewelry that belonged to her mother; pictures of her family in Poland. She even had her father's *tefillin*. And everything she showed me had a story to go with it. It was better than a movie! I asked her if I could bring Sammy to see her things too. Then Sammy's two sisters and Heddy came. Even Ezra would drop in if he was home. Mrs. Kirshen would prepare something before we arrived, and when we came it would be like a history lesson — but a *living* history lesson, not like some of the lessons we have in school!

But then Mrs. Kirshen got sick again, and two months later, she died. I felt awful.

A few weeks later, we got a phone call from Mrs. Kirshen's lawyer. He said that Mrs. Kirshen had written a will and left some of her things to me! We were all flabbergasted . . . me most of all!

Dad went down to get the things, and he came home with the old trunk from her bedroom. Inside were all of Mrs. Kirshen's 'treasures' — the coins; Mrs. Kirshen's *siddur*; the family pictures; the *tefillin*; the jewelry; and the most beautiful silver Chanuka *menora* I had ever seen.

I talked it over with Mom and Dad, and we all agreed that I should sell the jewelry and give the money to *tzedaka*. Zeidy took the *tefillin* to a *sofer* to repair them, and then we gave them to the

Old Age Home for the men to use. But I kept everything else. I put the pictures in my album, and every Chanuka when I light the *menora*, I think of Mrs. Kirshen.

Living Alone

The winter after Mrs. Kirshen died, I didn't feel like fooling around much. I was thinking about a lot of different things and I felt that I was really growing up. Even Zeidy said I was getting older every day.

The winter finally came to an end. Tu B'Shvat and Purim and Pesach came and went, until one day it was warm and sunny with a good, earthy, summery smell outside.

Everyone in school was fidgety. During recess some of us collected grasshoppers in the empty lot next to the schoolyard. Back in class, two of mine got out of my schoolbag and started hopping around the room. We hadn't started learning yet, so everyone ran around trying to catch the grasshoppers. Rabbi Lang thought it was pretty funny, but just then Rabbi Pane came in, and HE didn't think it was funny at all. Neither did my folks (Rabbi Pane called them, of course). They said I had to stay in after school for three days. Just when it was so nice outside too!

That was when I started thinking about moving. Danny kept saying he was going to rent an apartment with a friend some day and I was wondering how I could do something like that, but without waiting until 'some day.'

Just then Sammy called up and yelled into the phone, "Guess what! My folks are going on vacation for a few days and my sisters are staying with friends. If your parents will let you come here, we can stay all alone in my house!" Here I was wanting something impossible, and the next minute I had it. Life is full of surprises!

Sammy's mother left us a list of *Things to Do* and *Things to Make Sure Not To Do*. It was around three miles long. If we checked that list every day, we wouldn't have time to do anything else!

The first morning we were alone we got up nice and early to go to *shul*. When we came home, we decided to have chocolate sodas and pizza for breakfast. We felt like real adults, deciding on our own menus! We didn't have time to wash the dishes before school, but we piled them into the sink and went off like two kings.

In the afternoon we stopped off at the Koshermart. My mother offered to serve us supper, but we preferred shopping and cooking for ourselves. (Actually we didn't intend to cook much, but we had to pick up more pizza and ice cream.) Sammy said he thought it was silly to wash the dishes three times a day; we could just take turns washing them once a day in the evenings. I did him one better and said we should just keep piling them into the sink until we went through the whole set. Then we'd only have to wash every three or four days. So that's what we decided to do.

It was nice—for a while. No one telling us what to do. No cleaning up all the time. No garbage to keep taking out (we let that collect too; when the pail filled up or got smelly, we'd take it out). No one to send us to bed if we weren't tired. It was great.

But after a few days, I noticed this funny smell in the bedroom. At first it didn't bother me too much, but then it got bad. I started using a deodorant spray in the room, but it made Sammy sneeze (he has an allergy) so I had to stop. Finally I said, "Listen Sammy, either we find out what's smelling or else I'm gonna sleep in another room."

It turned out to be the socks. We had been piling up our dirty clothes in the corner of the room. I guess we should have put them in the dirty clothes hamper. I never knew that a dirty sock smell could be so strong. Sammy wasn't sure how to operate his washing machine and we didn't want to ask Mom to do our laundry, so we had to take the stuff to the laundromat and pay to have it done.

We were also having a little trouble in the kitchen. There weren't enough drinking glasses, so even though we didn't have to wash dishes very often, if we wanted to drink from a clean glass, we had to keep washing the glasses. But the glasses and the dishes were all mixed up in the sink. Every time we needed a glass we had to start pulling things out of the sink. We broke a few dishes this way and Sammy cut his hand and couldn't wash when it was his turn. So I got stuck doing this big pile of dishes alone all the time.

After a few days I also had a stomach ache from all the chocolate sodas and pizzas we were eating. I didn't ever want to see a chocolate soda or a pizza again, but Sammy said we had to finish eating all the ice cream and pizza we bought before his parents came back. I didn't see why we had to eat it all, but he said his mother would be angry if she saw how much we had bought.

The next thing I knew, Sammy was saying, "Listen, Jeremy, my folks are coming home tomorrow and we have to get this place cleaned up." We figured it would take at least a week to get everything back into place. But I was tired from staying up late every night, and I just COULDN'T start cleaning.

"Let's go to sleep early tonight and get up at five in the morning. Then we can have the whole place clean before we go to *daven*." That was MY suggestion. But Sammy was getting nervous. He wanted to clean NOW. I told him I didn't leave MY house to have to take orders in HIS house, and if that was how he was going to talk, I'd leave. He called me a fair weather friend—ready to mess his house up, but not willing to clean it. He said he'd clean the whole place alone.

I felt bad because Sammy and I hardly ever argue and this whole thing was stupid. Finally I said, "Listen, I'm so tired I can't see straight. Let's just go to bed. Tomorrow we'll get up early and stay home from school if we have to. We can spend the whole morning cleaning. Your parents won't get home until the afternoon."

So that's what we did. Rabbi Lang didn't like it one bit. Nor did Rabbi Pane. Nor did my folks. And each one let us know about it too! But we did get the house clean. It looked good as new.

Then I went home. It was Friday afternoon. My house never looked so great. Mom was cooking for *Shabbos* and it smelled delicious after all those chocolate sodas and pizza. My room didn't smell of dirty socks either, and our kitchen wasn't full of garbage. All the glasses were clean because we washed them after every meal. Even Heddy didn't look so bad when I first came home.

I guess being an adult and having to take care of everything yourself isn't all that it's cracked up to be. In fact, it's kind of tiring. I suppose that's why parents are always trying to get their kids to help them out. They must get tired of all the work they have to do. I decided then and there that I'd try to help my mom out more, now that I understood what she was up against. All things considered, she was doing a pretty good job. I told her so too, and she seemed pleased to hear me say it. In fact, she was so grateful that she wanted to do something nice for me. So Sunday afternoon when everyone was eating grilled cheese sandwiches (which I don't like), she came over to me and said, "Here Jeremy, I made you something you DO like." Then she handed me a chocolate soda and pizza!

✡ ✡ ✡
Baseball, Bar Mitzva and Spring
✡

For the last three seasons, our neighborhood baseball team always practiced on Monday and Wednesday afternoons. This spring, when we got together to start playing again, we had a problem. A couple of the kids had to take music lessons during the week, and some of them had jobs after school. So they decided to practice on Saturday mornings.

In our house, we do all sorts of things on *Shabbos,* but playing baseball is not one of them. Brian Kohn voted against practicing on Saturdays, because he knew that meant I couldn't be on the team anymore. The guys were willing to practice later in the day so that I could go to *shul* in the morning, but I explained to them that I couldn't play baseball ANY TIME on *Shabbos.* Baseball and *Shabbos* just don't go together. But they didn't understand why not (they don't go to Kerem HaTorah Yeshiva like I do). So I told them to go ahead and practice whenever it was convenient for them. I said I was kind of busy anyway this year. I'd have to start learning for my *bar mitzva* one of these days and I didn't think I'd have much time to play baseball. Then I resigned from the team.

Brian walked me home, but he was very quiet. Finally, he said, "Jeremy, I think you're great, giving up the team for the Sabbath. I know how much you like playing left field. It's really too bad you have to miss out on so many things because your family is so strict about the Jewish laws. Maybe when you're older, after your *bar mitzva,* you can join some synagogue that will let you play baseball on Saturdays." When Brian said that, I started to laugh. He means well, but he really has a lot to learn.

"What's so funny?" he asked me.

"You get the weirdest ideas," I answered. "I like my *shul* just fine. Besides, even if a Jew joins a different synagogue, he STILL has to keep the Sabbath!

"Just think, Brian, what's more important? A Holy Day that God Himself gave to the Jewish people thousands of years ago, or baseball practice with a few guys? We wait all week long for *Shabbos.* It's the best day of the week! Why don't you spend next *Shabbos* at our house? Then you can see for yourself!"

When I told all of this to Dad, he said it was another sign that I was growing up. He said that when a person is able to weigh things and make decisions, and to give up SOME things because

OTHER things were more important, that's a sure sign of maturity. He said he was sorry I had to leave the team, but he was proud I'd made the right decision all by myself. I felt good when Dad said that (even though I admit that for a minute or two in the afternoon I was feeling a little sorry for having to leave the team).

Then Dad said, "Your birthday is coming up, Jeremy. Maybe it's about time to have Zeidy start teaching you to read in the Torah. We might as well start early so you have plenty of time to practice. I'll speak to him tonight."

I gave Dad a big hug and ran into the kitchen. I tried singing a few notes, but my voice didn't sound so good, so I made myself an eggnog. (Mom calls it a 'goggle-moggle.' She says it makes the voice sound sweeter and it's good for the throat.) Then I sang a few more notes, but I didn't sound any better. I was going to try another eggnog when Zeidy himself walked in.

"What are you up to?" he asked.

"Sweetening up my voice so you can start teaching me to read in the Torah!" I answered.

So we both had an eggnog together and we went to work. And would you believe it? I learned all the *te'amim* perfectly in just one week!

Brian spent a *Shabbos* at our house and he

liked it so much that he asked us to invite his parents too. We did, and they were so interested in all the things Zeidy told them that they started thinking about sending Brian to the Yeshiva next year! Meanwhile, I'm teaching him the *aleph-beit* so he can learn to read.

It was near the end of the semester and things were pretty quiet in school. Everybody was sitting around waiting for vacation to start. Rabbi Pane stopped me once or twice in the hall and told me how well I was "living up to my potential" and how pleased he was. Rabbi Lang got married. He said he would be moving out of town next year, so he couldn't be our teacher anymore. I was sorry about that. I would have liked to see him around. It's always nice to talk to Rabbi Lang, even if he's not my teacher.

They skipped Heddy again and put her up into the third grade. She was the youngest girl in the class. I was glad I only had two more years to finish grammar school. If I were in a lower grade and they skipped Heddy a few more times, she would catch up with me! Just thinking about it gave me a headache!

Sammy was busy trying to build a model *Beit Hamikdash* in his garage (his parents got rid of the bathtub so there was room). He wanted me to help him, but I didn't feel like it. I was busy practicing my *parsha* every day and learning the laws of putting on *tefillin*. Dad said that on my twelfth birthday he would go to the *sofer* and order my *tefillin* because it takes a while until they are ready.

I waited for that birthday and it seemed like it would never come. But it did. That's one thing you can always count on. Time keeps moving, no matter what. Sometimes it goes by awfully slow, but whatever you're waiting for will get there eventually!

✡ ✡ ✡
Turning Twelve
✡

I was born on the 6th of Tammuz at 10:23 A.M. It's hard to imagine that only twelve years ago I was a tiny baby, and now I'm, well, not exactly grown up, but almost.

I'm too big for birthday parties, but I felt we should celebrate somehow. I told Mom and she said that since school was over, we'd all go to the State Park on the night of my birthday and the family would make me an outdoor celebration. We took our tent and the outdoor grill and lots of food. We had to pack so much stuff into the car that Dad said it looked as though we were going on a ten-week trek to the Himalayas instead of just on a picnic-dinner thirty miles from home.

Heddy didn't want to sit on the ground because she was afraid of snakes. Danny wanted to eat in a restaurant; he said it's more comfortable than eating out. But Ezra and Mom said that they were planning the trip and we had to do things their way. Danny was appointed General Camp Manager and Dad volunteered to be the cook.

Heddy was supposed to be Danny's assistant. Ezra and Mom took care of the program for the evening. I didn't have to do anything except make a speech in honor of the occasion.

We found a really neat place to camp, right next to a little stream. While everyone was busy with their jobs, I wandered off to think about my speech. After all, it's not every day that I become twelve!

I walked around, following the stream and thinking hard, when I saw a rabbit. I was walking very quietly and he didn't hear me. I thought it would be fun to see how long I could follow him before he ran away. He wandered away from the stream and hopped up a little hill and disappeared. I sat down for a while and waited to see if he'd come back, but he didn't. It was getting dark and I was getting chilly, so I turned around and went back down the hill to the stream, but the stream wasn't there! I figured I must have come down the wrong side of the hill by mistake (because streams don't just disappear), so I walked back around the bottom of the hill—three times! But I STILL couldn't find that stream. The sun was setting so I stopped to *daven mincha*, and then I walked around the hill again. The more I walked, the darker it got and the colder I became.

Finally, I was really scared. I called and called but no one answered. I couldn't understand how I could have walked so far away that my family couldn't hear me. I started thinking about those snakes Heddy was afraid of. I had laughed at her and told her there were no poisonous snakes around here, but now I wasn't so sure.

I KNEW I couldn't be too far from my family; the worst that could happen was that it would take them a few hours to find me. Maybe I'd even have to spend the night alone in the dark. But they'd surely find me in the morning, right? I mean, I KNEW they would! After all, I wasn't lost in a desert or a jungle or anything like that. It was only the forest preserves in the State Park!

I didn't want to start feeling sorry for myself. I was twelve now and I wasn't going to panic and act like a baby. But I did feel sorry for my mom. She'd be worried sick about me. Sometimes she was very sensible, but now she was probably thinking there were lions around ready to eat me or something, which was perfectly ridiculous! But I got a little upset worrying about her.

I began to wonder what if, by some oddball chance, they DIDN'T find me. Could someone die from exposure—or starvation—in a State Park? Would Heddy care, or would she just take all my books and stuff? Would anyone give some of my things to Sammy so that he'd remember me? Zeidy would be awfully unhappy if I wasn't around for my *bar mitzva*. It would spoil the whole day! I began to realize what a tragedy it would be if I died at such a young age! I got so involved in thinking about it that I started to cry a little.

I promised myself that if only someone found me, I'd never laugh at Heddy again. I wouldn't try to aggravate Danny anymore either. And I'd help my mom whenever she asked. I didn't even care if I had to keep sharing a room with Heddy. It just didn't seem so important anymore if I had my own room or not. Even Rabbi Pane didn't seem so bad!

I leaned up against a tree (I was afraid to sit down on the ground because by then it was dark. I couldn't see what I was sitting on and I kept thinking of Heddy and her snakes!) Zeidy says that whenever a Jew is in trouble, he prays to *Hashem,* so I prayed the hardest prayer I had ever prayed. "Please, *Hashem,* let someone find me! I want to be back together with my family!" And then I started to cry.

Next thing I heard (besides my own crying) was "JEREMMMY!" It was Danny! I was so happy I could have exploded! I called back, "I'm here. Over this way!" and I started running. Then I found the stream. I *knew* it was the stream immediately because I tripped over a branch and fell right into it.

When Danny came up with a flashlight, I jumped up, freezing and wet, and gave him the biggest hug he ever got from me!

"Let go! You're choking me! What's wrong with you? And why are you all wet?"

"I'm so glad to see you!" I said. "I thought you'd NEVER find me! It must be almost morning!"

"Morning? What are you talking about? We're waiting for you so we can eat supper. You've been gone for forty-five minutes."

I couldn't believe my ears! "Only forty-five minutes? You must be kidding. I've been wandering around here lost for hours and hours!"

Danny looked at me kind of funny. Then he gave me his jacket. "Maybe it felt like hours to you, but it was only forty-five minutes. I didn't even know you thought you were lost. I just came to call you back. Are you sure you're OK?"

I felt pretty silly, acting like such a baby when I was only lost for forty-five minutes! I guess I'm not as grown up as I thought I would be when I turned twelve. I hadn't even thought of looking at my watch to see what time it was!

"We don't have to tell anyone you thought you were lost," said Danny. "They'll just think you were out scouting around." That was the first time I can remember Danny being so considerate of my feelings!

When I finally got into dry, warm clothes, we had our meal. It was pretty good too. Dad never cooks at home, but he's great outdoors. He says it's his way of giving Mom a rest from the kitchen. Then Mom and Ezra put on their production. It was *This is Your Life—Jeremy Levi*. The two of them imitated every single person on the show—themselves, Dad, Zeidy, Danny, Heddy; Rabbi Lang and Rabbi Pane, and Brian; they even imitated me! They were great. That's what I like best about Mom and Ezra. They know how to act a little bit crazy sometimes, just so things don't get too dull in our house.

When it was my turn to give my speech, I realized that I'd been so busy getting lost that I hadn't prepared a single thing to say. Then I remembered my prayer by the tree. I didn't know that a prayer could get answered so fast, and I knew that I had to be thankful for it. So I asked for a few minutes to think, and then I said:

"Today I discovered something important. I used to spend a lot of time thinking about the things I wanted but didn't have, like a room for myself. Today I discovered how important it is to be thankful for the things I *do* have, especially when I already have the things I want most of all. I have all of you!"

We ate my birthday cake (I don't think twelve is too old for a birthday cake, do you?) and Dad announced that he had been to the *sofer* to order the parchments for my *tefillin,* and Zeidy had gone to order the *battim*—the black cases for the parchments.

Do you know what? My twelfth birthday was the best birthday I ever had!

Going on Thirteen

I had wanted to be twelve for a long time. I know there's only one year's difference between eleven and twelve, but there's a big difference between them just the same. You see, being eleven means you're still a kid. But twelve, well, that's the first step towards being grown up. On my NEXT birthday, I'll be *bar mitzva*. I'll be expected to take care of myself and keep all the *mitzvot*, just like an adult. It's a pretty responsible job! Of course I'll still have to listen to my folks, but I won't be a little kid anymore.

My parents said that if Zeidy goes to *Eretz Yisrael,* maybe I can go with him for a few months, so that's what I'm planning for next summer. It's pretty exciting, believe me! It'll give me something to think about all year long. When I have time to think, that is, because I'll be in the seventh grade after the summer, and that's not the same as sixth grade. The work is harder, and we get out of school an hour later.

And I AM growing up. It's taking a while, but I can feel it happening all the time. Two weeks ago when Heddy was running around, she bumped into me while I was carrying a glass of hot cocoa. She spilled it all over my good pants. My hand automatically picked itself up to give her a good slap, but then my head said, "Wait a minute. Don't slap her. She's just a little kid. She didn't mean to jam into you like a blind bat. She just wasn't careful. And you really can't expect a six-year-old to be as responsible as, say, a twelve-year-old!" So I didn't hit her. I just said, "Next time, look where you're going." She was so surprised I didn't hit her that she even apologized!

(Of course, yesterday was a different story altogether. She sat down right on top of the model airplane I had just worked on for four hours and she smashed the whole thing! That time I DID get good and angry! But she deserved it. The plane was on MY bed, and if she's going to sit on my bed, the least she can do is look before she sits!)

Mom said that in September Danny would be learning in a yeshiva out of town and he'll be staying in the dormitory. She wouldn't let him rent an apartment of his own after all. She said he's too young to be living all alone! I'll move in with Ezra and take Danny's bed. When Danny comes home on vacations, he'll sleep in the den. Ezra said it will be a pleasure to have me and I can read his books all I want as long as I don't take them out of the room. I think it'll be nice being in a room with Ezra, maybe even nicer than having a room to myself. That could be sort of lonely.

I was talking to Zeidy the other day, and I told him now that I'm twelve, I feel like a different person. He said that a person has to know who he is and that even if I FEEL different, I'm still the same Jeremiah Levi and I should never forget it.

I started wondering exactly who IS Jeremiah Levi, and I came to the conclusion that I'm a lot of different people all rolled into one. I'm Rabbi Lang's student and Sammy's best friend and Brian's pal. I'm Heddy's older brother and Danny and Ezra's kid brother; Mom and Dad's son, and Zeidy's grandson.

I'm Yirmiyahu ben Gershon haLevi, part of *Am Yisrael*, and I'm just plain me—Jeremy—all by myself!

Of course everyone is always wishing I would be different from what I am. Mom is always saying things like "If you only liked the piano as much as you like the drums."

Dad says, "If you only showed a little more interest in your studies."

Danny says, "If only you didn't ask so many questions all the time."

Ezra says, "If you could only stay out of trouble for a few days in a row."

Zeidy says, "If only you wouldn't dream quite so much!"

Sammy says, "If you would only dream up good ideas like the S & J Employment and Mitzva Agency more often."

Heddy is the funniest of all. She says, "If only you were a SISTER instead of a brother!" Poor Heddy! She's surrounded by boys. I guess she has her troubles too.

But if I were all or any of these other things, I wouldn't be me. Zeidy says *Hashem* made only one Jeremy Levi in the whole world and that no one else is exactly like me. And that's why I have to make sure I turn myself into the best person that I can possibly be.

Now that I'm twelve and I'm growing up, I'm awfully busy. I have a lot of work to do—learning all the *mitzvot* I have to keep, and keeping all the *mitzvot* I'm learning about! But I don't mind one bit. Personally, I think twelve is a great age to be.

Do you know why? Because it means that *b'ezrat Hashem*, on my next birthday I'll be thirteen. And thirteen means *bar mitzva*!

Glossary of Hebrew and Yiddish Words

aleph beit	the Hebrew alphabet
Am Yisrael	the Jewish people
bar mitzva	a Jewish boy who, at age 13, becomes obligated to perform the commandments
Baruch Hashem	Thank God!
Beit Hamikdash	the Holy Temple which was in Jerusalem
b'ezrat Hashem	with God's help
bikkur cholim	the commandment to visit the sick
birkat hamazon	the prayer after eating a meal
challa, challot	braided white bread for the Sabbath
Chevron	the city of Hebron
chumash	the Five Books of Moses
daven	to pray (Yiddish)
Eretz Yisrael	the Land of Israel
Galil	the Galilee: a section in the north of Israel
gam zu letova	"This, too, is for the good."
gemara	Talmud
gemillat chesed	kind deeds
Hashem	"The Name," a way of referring to God
Kever Rachel	Rachel's Tomb
kley zemer	musical instruments
klezmerim	musicians (Yiddish)
Kotel	*Kotel Hamaaravi,* the Western Wall. The only remaining part of the Second Temple
lashon hakodesh	the Holy Tongue, Hebrew
levi, leviim	the Levites, helpers to the Priests in the Temple

GLOSSARY

livyatan	the leviathan, a large sea animal
Mashiach	the Messiah
Me'arat Hamachpela	the Machpela Cave in Hebron, burial place of Abraham, Isaac and Jacob; Sarah, Rivkah and Leah
menora	a candelabra for Chanuka
mezuza	a parchment scroll inscribed with the prayer of *shema* and affixed to doorposts of Jewish homes
mincha	the afternoon prayer
minyan	ten men needed for communal prayer
mitzva, mitzvot	commandments; sometimes used to mean "good deeds"
Negev	the southern, desert-like section of Israel
parsha	the weekly portion of the Torah
Shabbos	the Sabbath (Ashkenazi pronunciation)
shacharit	the morning prayer
shnapps	whiskey (Yiddish)
shul	synagogue (Yiddish)
siddur	prayer book
simcha	joy, happiness
sofer	a scribe
sukka	the temporary hut Jews live in for eight days during the holiday of Sukkot
tallit	prayer shawl
Tammuz	the 4th month of the Hebrew year; corresponds approximately with July/August
te'amim	marks printed in the Hebrew Bible indicating how to read the Torah Scroll
tefillin	phylacteries
tehillim	Psalms, written by King David
tzedaka	charity
Yerushalayim	Jerusalem

Other Feldheim Young Readers Division books by YAFFA GANZ:

Hello Heddy Levi!
From Head to Toe: A Book About You
The Jewish Fact Finder: A Bookful of Important Torah Facts and Handy Jewish Information
Savta Simcha and the Incredible Shabbos Bag
Savta Simcha and the Cinnamon Tree
Savta Simcha and the Seven Splendid Gifts
Follow the Moon: A Journey through the Jewish Year
Who Knows One? A Book of Jewish Numbers
The Gift That Grew
The Terrible-Wonderful Day
The Story of Mimmy and Simmy
Shuki's Upside-Down Dream
Yedidya and the Esrog Tree
The Riddle-Rhyme Book

Yaffa Ganz lives in Jerusalem with her husband, four sons and one daughter. Many of her ideas come from her own lively family as she sees just how confusing and how funny growing up can be.

Mrs. Ganz's stories and articles have appeared in Jewish publications in Israel, the U.S., England and Canada. She has also written *Savta Simcha and the Incredible Shabbos Bag, Savta Simcha and the Cinnamon Tree, Who Knows One—A Book of Jewish Numbers, Follow the Moon—A Journey Through the Jewish Year, Yedidya and the Esrog Tree,* and *The Riddle Rhyme Book.*